Written by Rebekah Wilson
Illustrations by Jeffrey Wilson

Produced by:

FriesenPress
Suite 300 – 852 Fort Street
Victoria, BC, Canada V8W 1H8

www.friesenpress.com

Distributed to the trade by The Ingram Book Company

This project is funded by the Métis Nation of Ontario's Education & Training Branch. For more information, please visit www.metisnation.org

Dedications

I would like to dedicate this book in memory of my great grandfather Joseph Rudolph Couture who taught me so much about his own Métis heritage and made me proud of my own; my late aunt Marilyn whom the main character is named after; and, my late Uncle Bob who taught me so much about music.

Thank you to my grandmother Leora Wilson for her hard work and research tracing our family's Métis roots, for always believing in me and encouraging me to follow my dreams.

Thank you to the Métis Nation of Ontario for funding this project, for providing some of the information reflected in this project and for giving me pride in my heritage.

Thank you to my many supportive friends and family who made sure I never gave up on fulfilling this lifelong dream!

Disclaimer: The views expressed in The Tiny Voyageur are those of the author and do not necessarily reflect the views of The Métis Nation of Ontario.

Tiny slipper covered feet scurried across the wooden floor outside of the house's master bedroom.

"Grandma ...Grandpa ..." a quiet voice whispered as the door hinges creaked open. The 8-year-old stood, wrapped in a colorful flannel sheet. Grandma snuck quietly out of bed and picked up the little girl. She lifted her finger to her lips, mouthing a 'shhh' as they walked to the little girl's room. Grandma tucked her into her blankets and sat on the edge of the small bed.

"Is everything all right, Marilyn?" Grandma asked. "Did you have a bad dream?"

Marilyn smiled, shaking her head.

"Tell me a story, Grandma," said the little girl. "About your grandpa and grandma."

"My grandpa and grandma lived a very different life than I did, and especially different from the one you live," began Grandma. "They had to hunt for food, instead of going to the grocery store. They built their own houses out of trees, and stayed warm by campfires. They didn't travel in cars or airplanes. They walked and canoed across lakes, for miles ..."

Marilyn held tightly to her teddy bear, her eyes becoming heavy before fluttering shut. "Good night, Grandma. Love you."

Grandma stood up as silently as possible and turned off the light. "Goodnight, my Tiny Voyageur," she said.

It seemed like no time had passed when Marilyn opened her eyes and stretched. She looked around for her grandparents but they were nowhere to be found. Beside her were a crackling campfire and two grown men wearing fur coats.

Confused and frightened, she jumped up from beneath a heavy wool blanket and started to sob quietly.

"You're awake," said one of the men, his voice deep. He held out his hand slowly to her. "No need to be afraid. I'm glad that you're okay."

The little girl began to feel cold, suddenly noticing the soft white snow beneath her tiny feet.

Another man was holding a stick with a fish attached to the end, cooking it over the open flame.

"I'm cold. Where am I? Who are you?" she asked, and the man looked back at her puzzled. She stood up and walked around, curiously looking at everything.

One of the men offered her his jacket. She wrapped it around herself and sat down by the fire, pulling her knees tightly to her chest.

"My name is Joe. Joe Couture. And this is my friend James. What is your name?

"Marilyn," she said, her voice shaky and nervous. "I want to go home."

Joe smiled sweetly and sat down beside the little girl. "We will get you home soon. Promise."

The little girl felt as though she recognized him; his strong nose and light eyes reminded her of her grandmother.

When the food was all gone, the men began to pack their things and load up the canoe. Marilyn did her best to help, but was met by an impatient grunt from James. Fighting away tears, the little girl stood beside Joe and wrapped her arms around his leg.

Joe retrieved a small sash from his shoulder pack and draped it onto the girl's shoulder. He wrapped it carefully around her waist and tied the ends, its tassels hanging to her knees.

"That's not how you tie a scarf," the little girl said, giggling.

Joe smiled softly. "What you are wearing is called a sash. Do you see mine?" He gestured at his own, wrapped around his waist, holding onto some tools and trinkets.

The little girl nodded, smiling and adjusting her own sash proudly.

Joe lifted the little girl into the canoe and handed her a package. "Could you hold this for me, please? It's very important, but I think you can look after it," he said, smiling. The little girl giggled and held onto the package, guarding it with her life.

"Where are we going?" said Marilyn, tilting her head sideways like a curious puppy.

"To the trading post," said James gruffly. "We have an important trade to do so you must stay out of sight and out of mind." Marilyn slouched into her seat; her chin quivering as she fought away tears.

She sat in the middle of the canoe, Joe seated in front of her, and James in behind. They brushed the paddles softly across the water as the canoe began to move forward. Joe offered a tiny paddle to the little girl. Her chest puffed out with pride and she dipped it into the water. She jumped when it touched the water, but tried again. She stopped for a moment and looked at both of the men, watching how they were paddling.

"Shouldn't we be wearing life jackets? I can't swim very well."

James grunted in disapproval while Joe laughed a hearty laugh. He turned around in his seat and showed her what to do.

"You can't swim? Well, we will have to make sure not to tip the canoe then, won't we? Stay seated and don't wiggle too much," said Joe, ruffling Marilyn's hair with his hand.

As they reached a calm spot in the water, Joe and James stopped paddling and began singing a song.

Marilyn nodded her head, clapping with excitement. She swayed and listened carefully as the men began to sing.

Tet, nipol, zhnu pi pyii (zhnu pi pyii!)
Tet, nipol, zhnu pi pyii (zhnu pi pyii!)
Zyeu pi zarey pi bush pi nii.

"I don't understand that song. I learned French in school but that is a different language. What are you singing?" she asked, looking to Joe for an answer.

Joe smiled and the two men began to sing again, in English this time.

Head and shoulders, knees and toes (knees and toes)
Head and shoulders, knees and toes (knees and toes)
Eyes, ears, mouth and nose!

"The language we were singing in is called Michif, the language of the Métis people. I sing this to my children, two young girls and one young boy. My wife was pregnant when I left several months ago but I am sure she has given birth now."

"Don't you miss them?" the little girl asked. "I miss my dad when he goes away."

"Of course I do. But it is my job to trade and provide for my family," he said. The little girl patted Joe on the back gently and smiled.

When they reached land, Marilyn nearly tumbled over the canoe's edge. Joe caught her before she could fall into the water, lifted her safely to land and offered his hand to her. She looked at him shyly before taking his hand.

They stopped along the path to drink some water and snack on some moist berries. James pulled a wooden case from his backpack, opening it to retrieve a small instrument.

"That's a very small guitar. How will you play it?" Marilyn asked.

James shook his head and chuckled, resting the instrument on his shoulder and setting his bow on top of the strings.

"Do you miss your family?" Marilyn asked James, her head tilted curiously. James nodded, his expression softening.

"Would you like to try?" asked James, holding out the instrument to her. Hesitant at first, Marilyn accepted it and began to play while James guided her hand holding the bow.

"You're a natural," he said, smiling for the first time all day. Joe chuckled and smiled also.

After a walk that seemed to go on for miles, they reached the trading post and James grunted as he looked at the little girl. Joe and James walked into the wood cabin, leaving

Marilyn scared and alone outside. She waited and waited and waited. Tree branches crackled in the distance and Marilyn started to cry again, scared of what might be lurking in the forest.

"What's wrong? Are you all right?" asked Joe as he stepped out of the cabin door.

Marilyn jumped up and into his arms, comforted by his presence and strong hug. She shook her head, sniffling as Joe used his sleeve to wipe a tear from her cheek.

"I want to go home. Now, please."

Joe held the little girl and carried her down the trail. "You will be home before you know it."

It began to get dark. Joe and James set up camp in an area surrounded by trees. Joe set Marilyn down but she followed him closely as he lit a fire.

James sat down beside Marilyn and wrapped her up in his warm coat, striped with yellow, green and red.

"I don't think I can sleep. I'm afraid of the dark. And I don't have my nightlight. Or my teddy bear," she said, leaning her head on Joe's shoulder. In place of her favourite teddy, he handed her a fuzzy bear's paw to help her sleep.

"Close your eyes, Tiny Voyageur," Joe said, wrapping an arm around Marilyn's shoulders. *"Bonne nuit."*

"Bonne nuit," the little girl said in return, closing her eyes and holding tightly to the bear paw. Moments later she was fast asleep as the two men sang songs and jigged, a traditional Métis dance, long into the night.

When Marilyn awoke, she sat up looking for the two men but her only company was her favourite teddy bear. She stretched out her arms and in her hand found the bear paw. She smiled from ear to ear, realizing she had lived a magical moment and it wasn't just a dream after all.

"Good morning glory. How did you sleep?" said Grandma.

Marilyn hugged her grandma tightly. "Oh Grandma, I'm so happy to be home," she exclaimed.

Grandma laughed and kissed Marilyn on the forehead as the little girl fidgeted with the furry bear paw in her hands.

"Where did you get that, dear?" Grandma asked. "My Grandpa Joe had a bear paw just like that."

"Tell me about him. What did he look like, Grandma?"

"Well," Grandma began, smiling as she reminisced. "He had a very friendly face and the blackest beard and moustache you ever saw. He always wore a red sash around his waist ..."

Marilyn giggled to herself, hopping out of bed and skipping into the kitchen alongside her grandma.

"I wish you could have met him. I think you would have liked him a lot," Grandma said while setting the breakfast table.

The little girl smiled, holding the bear paw tightly to her chest. "I think so, too."

THE END

Glossary

Fiddle music: The fiddle has figured prominently in the lifestyle of the Métis people for hundreds of years. It is the primary instrument for accompanying the Métis jig. The famous 'Red River Jig' has become the centrepiece of Métis music. Since this European instrument was exceedingly expensive in early Canada, especially for grassroots Métis communities, many craftsmen learned how to make their own (Credit: www.metisnation.org).

Métis: Pronounced may-tee. The offspring or a descendant of a French Canadian and a North American Indian. For the National definition, please visit www.metisnation.ca.

Métis sash: Perhaps the most prominent symbol of the Métis Nation is the brightly coloured, woven sash. In the days of the Voyageurs, the sash was both a colourful and festive belt and an important tool worn by the hardy tradesmen, doubling as a rope when needed. Not only functional, the sash is colourful and identifiable as Métis apparel. The sash itself served as a key holder, first aid kit, washcloth, towel, and as an emergency bridle and saddle blanket. Its fringed ends could become a sewing kit when the Métis were on a buffalo hunt (Credit: www.metisnation.org).

Métis jigging: The Red River Jig, the unique dance developed by the Métis people, combines the intricate footwork of Native dancing with the instruments and form of European music. Often the Métis made their own fiddles out of available materials because they could not afford the European imports. Traditionally, dancing started early in the evening and would last until dawn. Witnesses were often dumbfounded by the energy and vitality evident during celebrations which was matched only by the long, arduous days of labour necessary to keep Métis communities running (Credit: www.metisnation.org).

Michif language: The Métis are a distinct Aboriginal people with a unique history, culture and territory that includes the waterways of Ontario, surrounds the Great Lakes and spans what was known as the historic Northwest. The citizens are descendants of people born of relations between Indian women and European men who developed a combination of distinct languages that resulted in a new Métis-specific language called Michif. In Ontario, Michif is a mixture of old European and old First Nation languages and is still spoken today by some in the Métis community. Efforts are underway to rescue and preserve this critical component of Métis culture (Credit: www.metisnation.org).

Voyageur: A Voyageur was a person who engaged in the transportation of furs by canoe during the fur trade era. Voyageur is a French word, which literally means "traveler".

About The Author and Illustrator

Rebekah Wilson, Author

Besides being the proud daughter to illustrator Jeffrey Wilson, Rebekah's greatest passions include sport, culture, youth leadership, journalism and music. Rebekah is a proud citizen of the Métis Nation of Ontario and a Sheridan Institute of Technology Alumni following her studies in Print Journalism at the Trafalgar Road Campus from 2007-2009.

In 2009, Rebekah worked as an editorial intern at the *Creemore Echo* before moving to Ottawa where she worked at the Métis Nation of Ontario as a registry and communications assistant. In 2010, Rebekah was chosen to be one of 350 Aboriginal youth from across Canada to dance in the opening ceremonies of the Vancouver 2010 Winter Olympics as well as take part in the Indigenous Youth Gathering.

Rebekah now works as the GEN7 Program Coordinator with Motivate Canada, an organization that specializes in improving the lives of young people by fostering civic engagement, social entrepreneurship, social inclusion and leadership among youth through sport and physical activity.

Jeffrey Wilson, Illustrator

Besides being the proud father to author Rebekah Wilson, Jeff's background includes being a cartoonist, illustrator, graphic artist and animator. He helped storyboard the classic 1980 Canadian film PROM NIGHT and was a key animator in the 1987 ADVENTURES OF TEDDY RUXPIN animated TV series.

In 1993, Jeff became an author himself, publishing SINCERELY CHORES: SKETCHES OF A FARM FAMILY, a collection of his AVRIDGE FARM weekly comic, which has appeared in community and farming publications across Canada. Jeff was on the council of the Grey-Owen Sound Métis Council in the late 2000s, where Jeff's mother and Rebekah's grandmother, Leora Wilson, served for many years as Senator.

CPSIA information can be obtained
at www.ICGtesting.com
Printed in the USA
LVHW070722170720
660848LV00001B/16